THE NEW KID

Uthman Hutchinson

illustrated by
Abdulmuttalib Fahema

First Edition
(1416 AH / 1995 AC)

© Copyright 1995 by The Children's Stories Project
555 Grove Street, Herndon, Virginia 22070-4705 USA

The New Kid and Other Stories
ISBN : 0-915957-45-0

Library of Congress Catalogue Card Number : 95-080049

Published by **amana publications**
10710 Tucker Street, Suite B
Beltsville, Maryland 20705-2223 USA
Tel: (301) 595-5777   Fax: (301) 595-5888

Printed in the United States of America by International Graphics
10710 Tucker Street, Beltsville, Maryland 20705-2223 USA
Tel: (301) 595-5999   Fax: (301) 595-5888

Contents

THE NEW KID

A new kid had entered school. His name was Anwar and he came from somewhere out of state. He even talked funny. He looked funny too. He had really short hair and big thick glasses with a colored elastic band attached to them behind his ears. He was extremely tall and thin and when the teacher called on him, he answered in a low voice that cracked.

"Nerd," whispered Muhammad to his friend, Daud, while the teacher was writing on the blackboard.

"Super Nerd!" Daud whispered back.

During recess Anwar wasn't chosen by anyone to play basketball so he just watched. After a while he got bored and wandered away. Later, when the other kids were waiting outside for the bus, Anwar waited inside. On the bus ride home he sat alone. His whole first week went the same way.

"He must have leprosy," said Daud that Saturday morning as he and Muhammad were walking to the store.

"No," said Muhammad. "It's probably something rare that contaminates the brain."

The boys laughed.

"You know he doesn't have a mother, don't you?" added Muhammad.

"Yeah," said Daud. "I bet they found him on a doorstep. He behaves like Sister Farida's his mom."

The boys had a good laugh at that one. Sister Farida was their math and science teacher and she liked Anwar a lot. In one week he'd proven himself the best student in both her classes. That hadn't helped his "nerd" reputation at all.

On the way back to Muhammad's house, carrying two packages of groceries, the boys decided to change direction and pass by Anwar's house. It was only a couple of blocks out of the way. They stopped at Anwar's house every day on the school bus but neither of them had walked past it since Anwar had moved in.

"If he's outside don't say a word to him," said Muhammad. "Just pretend he doesn't exist."

Daud agreed.

Anwar was outside. He was standing in his driveway shooting baskets. The boys could see him as they rounded the corner.

Anwar was just setting himself to shoot, standing a long way back from the basket, up by his garage. He launched the ball into a long curve. Swish! The ball didn't even touch the rim. Anwar retrieved the ball and set himself up in the same place again. The ball arched through the air. Swish again!

As the boys approached, Anwar continued taking three shots from each position, working his way clockwise around the basket. He was concentrating so hard that he didn't even notice the other two boys' arrival. He didn't miss a shot.

Now Muhammad and Daud were walking right past the driveway. They were watching Anwar, and as he picked up the ball beneath the net, he turned and saw them for the first time. He opened his mouth to say something but then didn't. The other two boys had already turned away and walked past, ignoring him.

First hurt and then anger showed in Anwar's eyes. He

dribbled the ball hard across his driveway and out onto his lawn. He whirled quickly and shot. This time the ball didn't swish. It went in like all the others, but only after rolling twice around the top of the rim.

At the end of the street Muhammad and Daud turned back to reexamine the boy they'd just slighted. Both boys felt bad but neither one would say so. Sometimes being mean felt good, even though you really understood it was wrong, but sometimes it just felt bad. This time it definitely felt bad. Neither boy looked at the other.

As they turned, Anwar was driving in towards the basket, dribbling from his garage. He gave the ball one last, hard bounce and left the ground. Up, up, up, he went, the hand with the ball stretched, his body seemed to be sailing. Then the ball cleared the rim and, Wham! It shot back down, slamming through the net.

Both boys stood perfectly still at the end of the street.

"Wow!" said Daud finally.

Anwar was driving up towards the net now from the downhill side. Up he went again and, Slam! He hit another perfect dunk! You could hear the rim bouncing all the way down the street to where the two boys stood silently.

Muhammad just turned and started to walk away. After a moment's hesitation, Daud followed.

"Did you see that?" said Daud. "He can dunk the ball!"

"Big deal!" said Muhammad. But Muhammad knew that it really was a big deal.

The guy could slam-dunk! He could set shoot like crazy

too, but the main thing was he could dunk the ball! Nobody in the whole school could dunk! Him, Daud, William and Lateef; they were the best on the court, but still, none of them even came close to dunking the ball! This was going to change everything. "Man," thought Muhammad. "This new kid isn't just a nerd, he's a disaster!"

Later that evening, after the Maghrib* prayer at sunset, Muhammad didn't stay at the mosque and play basketball like he usually did on weekends. Instead, he rode home in the car with his father.

"How come you didn't stay tonight?" asked Mr, Saeed.

"I don't know," said Muhammad. "I just didn't feel like it."

"Is anything wrong?" asked Mr. Saeed. It wasn't like Muhammad to miss a game with the older kids if he could help it.

"No," said Muhammad. "I just don't feel like playing."

In truth, Muhammad didn't feel like playing. He lay in bed that night, with his little brother, Jamaal, sleeping across the room from him, and tried to figure it out.

"Okay," he thought. "So I've been a real jerk to the guy, so what? He's the nerd. Yeah, well, not anymore, he's not. Not the way he can play basketball! Yeah? Well, even so, he's a nerd, and I don't like him. There's no rule that says you have to like somebody!" He continued thinking.

"Man, can he play basketball though! He's going to blow

---

* (Ma-Grib) A sunset prayer in congregation; one of five prayers a day for Muslims.

everyone away when he finally plays at school." Then a completely different idea hit him. "What about the tournament?" That was something to think about! They could even have a chance with Anwar playing.

"Maybe he won't play though," Muhammad thought. "He doesn't even come out at recess anymore. Maybe he doesn't think we're good enough for him.

"No," thought Muhammad. "He'll play, sooner or later he'll play all right.

"I could always make up with him and get him onto our team," he thought. "Man, would that blow everyone's mind!

"Sure," he thought sarcastically. "Talk about being hypocritical! First you despise him and then you make up with him just because he can dunk the ball!

"Aw, forget it!" he thought, turning over on his pillow. "I don't care! Just because you're Muslim doesn't mean you have to love everybody. So, I hate the guy. It's his bad luck if he's a nerd, slam-dunk or no slam-dunk!"

The next morning Muhammad had forgotten all about Anwar. After breakfast he planned to ride his bicycle down to the reservoir and called up Daud to go with him.

"Oh, I've got something else to do," said Daud.

"Well," said Muhammad. "If it's something better than the reservoir, maybe I'll come with you."

"No," said Daud. "I'm already doing it with somebody else."

"Oh," said Muhammad. "Okay, well, I'll see you on Monday."

"Okay, see you in school," said Daud.

"What was that all about?" thought Muhammad.

He tried to get Lateef to go with him but Lateef was already out when he called. Mustafa lived too far away, and Brian, from across the street, was already gone too. It was too late to catch anyone. He had thought Daud was going with him.

In the end Muhammad didn't want to go by himself so he just stayed around the house all day and didn't do much of anything.

Muhammad couldn't figure out why Daud had changed his mind. They had talked about going together the day before. Muhammad had taken it for a plan. He and Daud had been best friends forever, and sometimes friends just did weird things. Muhammad didn't think about it anymore until the next morning on the way to school.

When Muhammad entered the school bus that morning, Daud and Anwar were already sitting together. Instantly, Muhammad knew that they had been together the day before too.

Both boys looked up as Muhammad got on the bus, but he ignored them completely and passed straight through to the back.

"Traitor!" he thought, "Daud, you stinking traitor!"

Recess that day was even worse!

Daud and Lateef were the team captains. To everyone's surprise, Anwar was out on the court and Daud picked Anwar first. Lateef picked Muhammad and then they chose up the remaining boys.

From the beginning the game was one-sided. Muhammad already knew what to expect from Anwar so he concentrated on trying to keep him away from the basket. He stuck close to the other boy, trying to steal the ball and break up any plays before they got started. It wasn't much use. Muhammad was a little faster than Anwar and better at ball handling, but even so, he couldn't stop Anwar from taking those deadly outside shots.

While all the other boys seemed happily amazed at Anwar's skill, Muhammad just found himself getting madder and madder. He could see the idea of new possibilities dawning on everyone's faces. He could see them all imagining victory at the city-wide mosque tournament with Anwar on their team. Watching that thought suddenly dawn on the others somehow made things even worse for Muhammad.

In his desperation to stop the other boy he started playing too rough. Even Muhammad's own teammates began telling him to take it easy and twice he was called on fouls. A couple of times both boys went up for rebounds and hit hard in the air.

"He's not as skinny as he looks!" thought Muhammad after they'd hit the second time. His shoulder and chest ached from the contact. "He's not fast though," he thought, "I can stop him."

If Muhammad had stopped to examine his feelings, he would have realized that he meant "stop him", not just in the game, but in the school in general. He probably would have been surprised at himself. It really wasn't like Muhammad at all. He was in the heat of the game though, and in his own rising anger, and the grudge that was forming, he didn't stop to think.

Now Anwar was open, coming in towards the basket. Muhammad somehow got himself there in time to challenge the other boy. The instant Anwar's eyes went up, Muhammad left the ground. He was in the air a split second before Anwar, and as the hand with the ball stretched toward the rim, Muhammad smashed both his hands down hard against the ball. At the same moment two things happened. The ball was knocked out of Anwar's hand and straight into his face, and the two boys collided in the air.

Both boys hit the ground hard. Muhammad's elbow was badly scraped, his shirt torn and bloody. Anwar's glasses were broken.

Muhammad was up in a second. He pushed the new boy back against the chain link fence. He wanted to kill him! Then, for the first time, there was a reaction. Anger flowed into Anwar like a flood and his hand went up in a fist as he came bouncing off the fence.

William jumped on Anwar from behind, dragging him back toward the fence again. Lateef grabbed him around the shoulders from the front, pinning his arms, shouting, "Hold it, cool down! Cool down!"

Muhammad was being dragged backwards by one arm, and then from around the chest by Mustafa. Then Daud was right in Muhammad's face, pushing him back against the chest and shouting, "What did you do that for?"

Suddenly, Muhammad wanted to fight Daud too. "You traitor!" he shouted.

Then Brother Umar was in between the boys. He got

Muhammad and Anwar by their shoulders, squeezing hard enough to really hurt. He shook them and stood them up, side by side against the fence.

"Shaytan* is laughing in your faces!" he said. "The Devil's laughing at you and now he's laughing at all of us!" He stared at the two boys, looking as angry as they had looked a moment ago.

"I want to see you two big shots upstairs in that prayer line together! You got fifteen minutes till prayer time. Then I want to see you two in that line, and I mean shoulder to shoulder, like brothers!" He let his words sink in for a moment.

"Now, if you can't stomach that, we'll see how you can stomach a trip to the principal and suspension and explaining that to your folks when they have to come in and pick you up!"

Brother Umar lifted Muhammad's arm and looked at the elbow. "You get inside and get that taken care of," he said. "And you," he said to Anwar when Muhammad had left. "You go wash for the prayer and cool yourself off."

That day, waiting for the bus after school, there wasn't any basketball. Brother Umar had forbidden it indefinitely. There would be no basketball again until Muhammad and Anwar decided to make up and were willing to play on the same team.

_____

* (Shy-Tan) Satan.

10

THE NEW KID II

Driving home from the sunset prayer, Muhammad was unusually quiet in the car. He knew that his father had heard all about the trouble on the basketball court that afternoon. Brother Umar and his father had sat together talking for a long time after the prayer.

Now, sitting in the front seat beside his father, with his younger brother and sister in the back seat, Muhammad dreaded having to tell his father about it.

"I hear that the basketball games have been cancelled," said Mr. Saeed.

"Yes," said Muhammad, staring out his window.

"Muhammad got into a fight today," said Fatima in a tattle tale voice.

"He almost got massacred!" added Jamaal.

"That's enough," said Mr. Saeed. There was a long pause while he waited for Muhammad to say something. Muhammad was waiting too though, and he outlasted his father.

"Do you want to talk about it?" asked Mr. Saeed.

"Not really," said Muhammad. There was another pause.

"Okay," said Muhammad's father, "but you're going to have to work this out. You know that. You've got three days to do it."

Muhammad nodded his head but didn't speak. His father left the subject and started talking to his brother and sister.

Muhammad felt trapped. He knew the Prophet Muhammad's saying about three days. "It is not permissible for a Muslim to shun his Muslim brother for more than three nights, that is they meet, and this one turns away and that one turns away. The better of the two is the one who says the greeting

11

first." He also knew his father's tone of voice. Sometimes his father would get angry and yell but that always passed quickly. That was not such a big deal. Sometimes his father was quiet though, with a particular kind of quiet. That meant something altogether different. When Muhammad's father quietly said you had to, "work it out" or "take care of it", that meant it was important, very important, and you'd better get it right!

"What a mess!" thought Muhammad.

To make things even worse, later that night Daud called on the telephone. At first Muhammad didn't want to come and take the call, but he changed his mind. Maybe Daud wanted to apologize.

"Why are you always so hard headed?" asked Daud. He was trying to be reasonable, Muhammad could tell from his voice. "We all treated Anwar badly, but at least the rest of us admit it! Why did you have to start a fight?"

This conversation was not going the way Muhammad had expected and it was making him angry.

"You're all just thinking about the tournament," he said bitterly. "You're all acting like a bunch of hypocrites!"

"Yeah, we're thinking about the tournament, all right," said Daud in retaliation, "and you know what? We're thinking about Anwar too. He's already twice the friend you ever were!"

"Yeah, well you are a traitor!" shouted Muhammad, but the line was already dead and he was only shouting at an empty receiver.

The next morning, even despite his anger, Muhammad was almost ready to swallow his pride and make up with everyone. Why wait the full three days? After all, he had been backbiting. All he had to do was admit it was his fault, even if he didn't really believe it. Then he would only have to put up with Anwar on his team for a few days and it would all be over. How hard could it be?

When Muhammad actually got on the bus, though, and he saw Daud and Anwar sitting together, his anger rose up again. He kept thinking about the phone conversation of the night before. "So, I'm only half the friend he is," he thought.

At school, Muhammad found that it wasn't just Daud who was giving him the cold shoulder. All the sixth grade boys were ignoring him, even Lateef.

"They must have worked it all out by telephone last night," thought Muhammad. "So, that's the kind of friends they are! They'll turn on you in a second!"

He knew exactly what they were doing. They were trying to punish him into apologizing just so they could play basketball again.

"Well, I can make them sweat too!" he thought. "I've got three days to play with, and they're not the only ones who can punish someone!"

As he thought that, Muhammad felt a kind of pride. He would stand against all of them! Whatever they could dish out, he would serve right back to them! He would make peace on his terms, when he wanted to!

At lunch time Muhammad sat outside on a bench alone. All the others sat together except for Lateef who hadn't come out yet. When Lateef did come out he paused for a moment, looking at the other boys and then at Muhammad. Then Lateef walked casually over to where Muhammad was sitting.

"Mind if I sit down?" he asked.

"Suit yourself," said Muhammad.

The two boys ate side by side for a couple of minutes, completely ignoring each other.

"You know, this is stupid," said Lateef finally.

"So?" said Muhammad.

"So?" said Lateef sarcastically. "What do you mean, 'So'? So let's quit being stupid! If this goes on much longer we're liable to loose basketball altogether and get ourselves cancelled right out of the tournament!"

What Muhammad was thinking was, "We won't get cancelled. I'll end this thing before that, but I'll end it, not you all." What he replied was, "Sure, and the tournament's suddenly such a big deal because you've got a star now and you figure you can win."

"Look," said Lateef. "All of us acted like idiots to Anwar. But we were wrong. Can't you admit you were wrong?"

"How about you all," said Muhammad. "How about how you're treating me?"

"Okay, so we're all wrong. So, what are we going to do about it?"

"You do something," said Muhammad. "I'm just fine!"

"Man, I don't understand you," said Lateef. "You love basketball. We're all friends, and Anwar's a really good brother! Why do you want to ruin it all? Why don't you just make peace; Anwar's willing, everyone's willing. Why make it hard on everybody?"

Lateef was right, and underneath his anger Muhammad knew it. It was stupid to make it this hard on everybody. They weren't exactly making it easy themselves though. Still, it was probably better to just make peace and get it over with. For the second time in the same day, Muhammad found himself almost ready to give in.

Muhammad nodded his head that he had heard Lateef.

"Okay," he thought. "I'll finish it today. After school I'll

14

go over to Anwar's and make peace."

Lateef went back and joined the others, and Muhammad finished his lunch alone. After a few minutes Muhammad threw away his trash and stood up to go inside. As he approached the other boys he almost stopped right then and extended his hand. An instant before Muhammad actually stopped though, something happened which changed everything.

"... a sore looser."

"He thinks he's so great."

The overheard words hit Muhammad like a whiplash! They were talking about him! The hurt came instantly with anger flooding right behind.

"Those hypocrites!" he thought. Now they were backbiting him! Two days ago they were chewing Anwar's flesh and now they were working on him! Well, forget them all! They could go a hundred years before he would make up with them!

Muhammad walked right past the other boys without showing anything on his face, but he was boiling inside. Then, for the first time, the idea hit him as an actual possibility that he didn't have to make up at all. He had that power. If he wanted, he could never make up. He could destroy their hypocritical friendship and their hypocritical tournament just by outlasting them all!

Throughout the afternoon Muhammad stewed in his resentment and anger. He had never been so deeply furious for so long and by evening he felt completely worn out by it. He kept bouncing between resentment at his friends' behavior and then remorse at his own. As the anger finally wore out of him, Muhammad found himself wondering what was really going on. How had things gotten to this point? The whole episode was like some crazy roller coaster that Muhammad was trapped on. The roller coaster kept shooting around and ending up in a worse place than the one it just left. Now Muhammad was actually becoming afraid of where it would take him next. He had to get off!

Muhammad was sitting in his room staring at his homework but not seeing it. His brother, Jamaal, had finished his homework and gone outside long ago.

Through his thoughts, Muhammad heard his father arrive home and make his way slowly through the house. He heard him stopping here and there on his way upstairs. Then his father looked around Muhammad's open door.

"Assalaamu Alaykum,"* he said.

"Wa Alaykum Assalaam," replied Muhammad.

"Have you made up with your friends yet?" asked Mr. Saeed.

"No," mumbled Muhammad.

Mr. Saeed came into the room and closed the door. "I don't know if you want my advice," he said, "but I'm going to give it to you anyway." He sat down on Muhammad's bed.

He looked at his son's unhappy face and sighed.

"I recognize a lot of myself in you," he said. "You and I both have inherited a stubborn streak that runs a long way back through our family. Your great grandfather was famous for it. I can tell you from experience that being extremely stubborn is going to be your worst enemy in life. That and anger, but everyone has anger. Not everyone's as stubborn as you and I are."

Mr. Saeed paused. Muhammad was listening but he wasn't looking at his father. "That's it," said Mr. Saeed, "end of

---

* Peace be upon you, the Muslim greeting and goodbye.

lecture."

Now Muhammad looked at his father. "That's all?"

"That's all."

Muhammad thought for a moment. "But you always said Great Grandpa's stubbornness was his best quality."

"That's right," said Mr. Saeed. "Without it we wouldn't have had our land in Pakistan. It would have been stolen from us."

Muhammad looked puzzled.

"Stubbornness is probably your best quality too," Mr. Saeed added. "But it sure isn't right now."

Muhammad thought he saw what his father was driving at.

"Look," said Mr. Saeed. "If somebody tried to make you give up worshipping Allah,* would you do it?"

"No," said Muhammad.

"What if they fought you?"

"I'd fight them back."

"What if they beat you, I mean, completely defeated you?"

"They couldn't," said Muhammad. "I wouldn't give up."

"That's what I'm talking about," said Mr. Saeed. "Stubbornness for what God loves is the best thing about you. When you're stubborn just for yourself, you've got a problem."

"But they're wrong too!" said Muhammad.

"Of course they are," said Mr. Saeed. "That's not the point."

"Then, why should I be the one to give in?"

Mr. Saeed smiled. "Stubborn," he said. "You give in

---

* God.

17

because you're wrong, not because they're right."

Muhammad didn't have an answer for that one.

"You know why the Prophet said three days, don't you?" Mr. Saeed continued. "It's because in three days things can't get too out of hand. The Arabs were famous for blood feuds, though it can happen anywhere. That's just human nature."

"The McCoys and the Hatfields," said Muhammad.

"Right," said Mr. Saeed, "American history. That feud went on for generations. When you have to make peace within three days though, it cuts off the cycle before it really gets started. It's like an automatic cut-off valve to keep people from going too far."

Muhammad understood exactly what his father was talking about, but somehow that didn't seem to make his situation much easier. The thought of turning around and apologizing and taking all the blame seemed awful, even hypocritical. "How am I supposed to make peace now, after everything that's happened between us?" he said more to himself than to his father.

"It's the practice of the Prophet to do it with a gift," said Mr. Saeed. "Try it. It helps take away the bitterness on both sides."

Muhammad thought long and hard that night about what his father had said. Finally he decided to just give up. He'd surrender and make peace. As soon as he really accepted the idea he found a kind of peace already descending on his heart. It really wouldn't be that bad after all.

Now Muhammad began to think about what kind of gift he could give Anwar. The more he thought about it the more he realized it would have to be something for the others too. That was a hard one to figure out, but Muhammad found himself

18

getting excited about the prospect. He'd have to make it really good, a gift that meant something.

It took an hour, lying in bed awake, before Muhammad finally came up with the perfect thing. He had a little money saved and he was sure his father would lend him the rest. He'd have to get his father's help to get it completed the next day, but he was sure it could be done.

For the first time in days Muhammad felt content with himself, but there was one more thing he wanted to do. Quietly, he went down the hall to the bathroom and washed for the prayer. Then he came back to his room and closed the door. The sound in the quiet room was his little brother breathing heavily in his sleep. Muhammad faced toward Makkah* and calmed himself to begin the prayer.

After he was done praying, Muhammad sat on the floor thanking Allah for showing him a way out. Then he asked God to accept what he was going to do the next day and to make real peace between himself and the other boys. Then he asked Him to never let him get on that roller coaster again!

The next morning when Muhammad got on the bus for school both Daud and Anwar glared at him. Muhammad didn't look back at them though. Now was not the time to say anything.

When they got off at school Muhammad took Anwar by the arm before the other boy could go inside. Anwar turned toward Muhammad with a questioning look.

"Can I speak to you for a second?" asked Muhammad.

Anwar let himself be led over to the benches. There they

---

* A city in Arabia where the Prophet Abraham built the first house of worship. Muslims face toward that house when they pray.

19

stood talking while other kids passed them by on the sidewalk. Daud stood waiting beside the mosque door and watched, not knowing what to expect.

"I want to apologize," Muhammad began. His heart was pounding and he was nervous. Why was that first sentence so hard to get out? "Stubborn!" he thought.

"I'm really sorry," he continued. "I was rotten to you, we all were; and I'm sorry about starting the fight."

"That's okay," said Anwar, but his eyes were not at all friendly.

"I'm not just saying this because of the basketball tournament," said Muhammad. "That is a part of it, I guess," he added, trying to be honest. "Anyway, if it's possible, I'd like to start all over again and not be such a jerk this time."

Muhammad extended his hand and Anwar took it with a good strong grip.

"That's okay with me," he said.

Muhammad could see from Anwar's face that he was still holding himself back, being wary. They had all treated him badly, especially Muhammad. Just words weren't going to patch things up immediately, but at least there was a start.

That day while Muhammad was in school, Mr. Saeed was at his office trying to arrange for the gift. He had to call five different companies before he finally got one that could do such a rush job. The company would have things ready by two-thirty and Mr. Saeed thought he could pick up the gift and get it to the mosque before school let out. As it happened Muhammad had already gathered all the sixth grade boys on the basketball court when Mr. Saeed arrived.

"Assalaamu Alaykum," said Mr. Saeed, and the boys returned his greetings.

"Bismillah,"* he said and handed Muhammad a flat, rectangular box. "The man says he can finish them any time. All he needs is half a day's notice." He patted Muhammad on the arm.

"I've got to get back," he said, and before Muhammad could even thank him, he waved to the other boys and returned to his car.

All the boys crowded around Muhammad as he opened the box. Inside it were matching basketball jerseys for all the sixth grade boys.

The jerseys were dark green with writing across the fronts in two curved lines of gold letters. The writing said, "AL-AZIZ", and beneath that, "BASKETBALL". Large gold numbers were printed on the backs.

Muhammad handed each boy a jersey and took one for himself. When he was done there was still one left in the box. Muhammad opened it up and turned it around to show the back. Under the number on this one was written, "ALL CITY CHAMPS".

"God willing," said Muhammad, "this is what they'll all say the day after the tournament."

That evening Muhammad hurried through his homework. Just as Mr. Saeed arrived from work, Muhammad was heading out the door with his basketball tucked up under his arm.

"Where are you going?" called Mr. Saeed.

"I'm going over to Anwar's to practice," said Muhammad.

"Be back in an hour!" called Mr. Saeed, but Muhammad was already running down the street.

---

* In the name of Allah.

21

When he went inside, Mr. Saeed found his wife looking through the kitchen window, watching their son disappear around the corner of the neighbor's house.

"He's so big now," she sighed. "He's growing up."

Mr. Saeed nodded. "Yes," he said. "He's becoming a man."

GRANDMA'S DEATH

Grandma had been in the hospital only three days when she died. It happened late at night and Muhammad didn't know it until the next morning at Fajr. His father woke him and they did the prayer together with his mother following. His father looked somehow different to him and very tired, and in the middle of the prayer he cried.

Muhammad had seen his father cry before a couple of times, but except for once, it had always been silently in the prayer, just a few tears welling up out of his father's eyes because he was so moved by the Quran* that was recited. This time was different. His father began to recite the Quran in a shaky voice and had to stop often. Twice he broke down and sobbed. That was when Muhammad realized his grandmother was dead.

After the prayer Mr. Saeed made dua** in a shaky voice for his mother; that Allah would forgive her anything she had done wrong and enter her into the Garden. Muhammad found that tears were welling up out of his own eyes and his voice was shaking too as he said, "Amin, amin." It was so strange; he couldn't believe she was dead, and to see his father like that; he felt somehow shifted from his foundation, scared.

---

* The Muslim Holy Book.

** (Do-Ah) A private prayer, asking Allah for something.

Mrs. Saeed put her arms around Muhammad. Grandma died late last night," she said.

Muhammad nodded his head. He felt numb, like it wasn't all quite real. The first thing he could think of to say was to his father. "I'm sorry, dad."

Mr. Saeed smiled dryly and squeezed his son's leg just above the knee. He had wiped the tears from his face and his voice was steady now. "It's all right," he said. "She's all right now." He patted Muhammad's leg and stood up. He put his hands in his pockets then and for an instant looked completely lost. He seemed so incredibly sad as he wandered into the kitchen, that it scared Muhammad. He had never seen his father look anything like that before.

Mrs. Saeed had been watching Muhammad. She hugged him again. "It's all right," she said, and she smoothed some hair across Muhammad's forehead. "There won't be any school today," she said.

Muhammad nodded. He knew the funeral would be today, that you were supposed to bury the dead as soon as possible.

Mrs. Saeed stroked Muhammad's hair. "Go on upstairs and get dressed," she said, "then come down and have breakfast with us. There's going to be a lot of work and we'll need your help. We'll let the others sleep for now."

As Muhammad went upstairs, he looked back and saw his mother go into the kitchen and put her arms around his father.

Later he and his parents sat at the dining room table. Mr. Saeed had a list of things to do in front of him. Muhammad had never realized there were so many things to take care of when someone died. It seemed terribly unfair.

At pauses in the conversation, Mr. Saeed would suddenly sigh and look down at the piece of paper. Then he would gaze away and get a strange expression on his face, as if nothing meant anything to him, as if everything were bitter. Mrs. Saeed kept her hand on her husband's hand on the table. Sometimes she would take his hand in both her hands and stroke it.

Uncle Hamza telephoned and said he would be coming to the house in half an hour. Mrs. Saeed got up to make breakfast. Mr. Saeed couldn't eat. Muhammad was upset about his grandmother and deeply shaken by his father's reaction, but somehow it seemed to make him more hungry. He ate two eggs and toast and then his mother made him more toast and jam.

Mr. Saeed had tried all night to telephone his sisters in Pakistan, but there was no one home. Now he phoned his uncle and aunt instead. When he was done talking, he wandered out into the living room.

Mrs. Saeed reached down and rested her hand on Muhammad's shoulder. Muhammad felt like he was stuffing his face, but he couldn't stop.

"Don't worry," said Mrs. Saeed. "Everything's all right. Grandma was a good woman and, inshallah*, she'll be in the Garden. Your father will be all right too, but it's hard. It's very hard when your mother dies. It's hard to loose your parents."

Mrs. Saeed's words hit Muhammad with a jolt. He knew they were meant to reassure him, but now he was really shaken. Everybody's mother dies. His mother was going to die. His father was going to die, any day! It felt like a huge, dark space

---

* God willing.

27

was opening up in his chest. Muhammad kept on chewing mechanically, staring straight ahead. What do I do, run away and scream? He realized after a moment that his mouth was empty. His mother gave his shoulder a squeeze and went upstairs to check on his sister and brother. Muhammad put down his toast and forced himself away from that dark, empty space.

He stared at his plate.

Muhammad knew about the Fire and the Garden. He knew about the questioning in the grave and the balance, the judgement of good and bad actions after death. It all pertained to him. He knew that. He accepted it. None of that bothered him. He knew about the afterlife. He knew that it was true and he trusted in it. He was used to talking about it and reading about it in the Quran. The contemplation of death was recommended by the Prophet. As a Muslim, the fact of death already formed the basis for Muhammad's keeping himself straight in this world. You had to keep straight because of it. But somehow Muhammad had never thought of his parents dying, not in concrete terms. That indisputable fact was suddenly forced upon him. It had to happen sometime and he couldn't stop it. He couldn't imagine living without them.

Muhammad stared at his half eaten toast. He felt he understood his father's reaction now. But he was a grownup. Didn't that make a difference? He thought about his father's crying and remembered the first time he'd seen him cry like that.

The whole family had gone to Grandma's hospital room to visit. She looked old and tired, propped up on the strange hospital bed. She said something to their father that Muhammad didn't hear, and then she smiled at the three children and motioned them over.

"Are you Grandma's boy?" she asked Jamaal.

"Yes," replied Jamaal, not as loudly as usual.

"Then give me a hug," said Grandma, leaning down so Jamaal could get his arms around her.

"You be a good boy and do what your parents say."

She kissed Jamaal on the cheek and smoothed back his hair. The hospital room with Grandma in that bed made Jamaal more subdued than usual. He just managed to mumble out the question on his mind.

"Can you come home tomorrow, Grandma?"

"We'll see," said Grandma. She put her other arm out toward Muhammad's sister, Fatima. Fatima was just on the verge of crying as she hugged her grandma.

"Don't cry, kitten," said Grandma. Kitten was her special name for Fatima and she said it in Urdu*. "Billa, Grandma's fine," she said as she stroked Fatima's hair. "Everyone gets sick sometimes."

Fatima's face was buried in the bedclothes and Grandma continued to stroke her hair. "Are you going to help your mother while I'm away?" Fatima kept her face buried, but nodded, yes.

Grandma looked at Muhammad. "You're almost a man," she said, "and you're going to help your father to protect your family."

"Yes," said Muhammad.

Grandma nodded. She looked more tired than ever. She smiled. "Give me a kiss," she said.

Muhammad leaned over his sister and kissed his

---

* The national language of Pakistan.

grandmother on the cheek. She smelled different than usual, like medicine. She kissed him back, very lightly, and as he stood back up she said, "Remember your prayers."

Then she lay back, looking completely exhausted. Her eyes were closed. "Good night, children," she whispered.

Mrs. Saeed leaned over the bed and took her mother-in-law's hand and kissed it. Then she began to herd the children out of the door. Muhammad was the last one out, and as he passed the foot of the bed he looked at his father. Tears were running down his father's face. Then he gasped and a huge sob escaped as if he had been trying desperately to hold it in. Then he began to really cry. Muhammad was stunned. Outside the door, Mrs. Saeed was already hurrying the children down the hall.

"What's wrong with daddy?" asked Jamaal in a frightened voice.

"Mama!" cried Fatima.

Both children tried to turn back, but Mrs. Saeed gently but firmly moved them towards the waiting room.

"Don't worry," she said. "Daddy's just upset because Grandma's sick."

Muhammad only now realized why his father had cried. He had known for sure that his mother was dying.

Muhammad glanced up from his plate. Uncle Hamza had arrived. He and Mr. Saeed finally reached their sisters in Pakistan and then things began to speed up. There were more phone calls, coming and going. Fatima and Jamaal came downstairs with their eyes red from crying. Fatima began to cry again at breakfast and had to go sit with her mother in the living room. Jamaal kept asking questions like, "When will we see Grandma again?" and "Why did Grandma get sick anyway?"

Finally he asked, "Why did Grandma have to die?"

"Finish your egg and come sit with us in the living room," said Mrs. Saeed, "We'll talk all about it."

Jamaal didn't want to finish his egg, though. He wanted an answer.

Mr. Saeed told Muhammad to get ready to go.

Muhammad went upstairs for his jacket. As he passed his mother, sitting on the couch with Jamaal and Fatima snuggled up against her, it struck Muhammad that they all used to snuggle up against their grandma in just that way. When he thought that, he hurried upstairs, so no one would see him cry. He heard his mother telling Jamaal, "You're going to see Grandma again sooner than you think."

Muhammad waited upstairs, wiping his eyes. He waited so long that his father had to call him to hurry up.

"Coming!" Muhammad called back. He blew his nose and put on his jacket.

When Muhammad came down, Jamaal had already gotten bored with his mother's explanations. He was in the middle of the living room playing with his trucks. Mrs. Saeed didn't usually let Jamaal play with his trucks there, but she allowed him that day. Jamaal was crashing his trucks together very hard. Fatima was still on the couch with her mother. Muhammad followed his father and uncle outside.

Uncle Hamza was going to the mosque and then the funeral home. Muhammad and his father had to pick up the things Mrs. Saeed would need later that morning to wash the body. They would get the things for washing in one store. They would get some towels and the clean, white sheets, for wrapping the body in another.

"We'll have to get some quick foods too," said Mr. Saeed. "A lot of people will come to visit, there won't be much time to cook." Then he became silent again and sighed loudly.

Muhammad wanted desperately to do something for his father, but he didn't know what to say or do.

"Grandma's all right," he finally said.

"I know," said Mr. Saeed. "I know." His voice became strained on the last sentence and he grimaced. Then he sighed again. They drove on in silence. Then Mr. Saeed said, "You can never serve your parents enough, Muhammad. Especially your mother . . . there's no way we can possibly repay what we owe."

Usually when someone said this Muhammad took it as an admonition. Now, though, his father was speaking about himself and his own mother. Mr. Saeed regretted not having done enough for Grandma. Muhammad was shocked.

"But, you did everything for Grandma," he said.

"But not enough," said Mr. Saeed. "I should have done more."

"But you did everything," Muhammad repeated, "you and Uncle Hamza."

Mr. Saeed patted his son on the knee. "I know," he said. "We did a lot." Still, Muhammad could tell that his father hadn't changed his opinion at all.

But if he hadn't served Grandma enough, how could anyone serve their mother enough? His father had loved Grandma. She had lived with them. He had fed her, clothed her and traveled with her back to Pakistan when she stayed there for part of the year. Every year he flew with her all the way to Pakistan just to drop her off and then come back alone after a few days' visit. Uncle Hamza had always picked her up when she was ready to return. His father even took Grandma to Hajj[*]! Then Muhammad remembered a Hadith[**] about a mother's position with her child.

"A person came to the Messenger of Allah, peace be upon him, and asked: Who among the people deserves the best treatment from me?

He said: Your mother.

The person asked: Then who?

He said: Again your mother.

The person asked: Then who?

He said: Again your mother.

The person asked: Then who?

He said: Then it is your father."

Muhammad decided Mr. Saeed was right, you could never do enough.

After an hour, Mr. Saeed and Muhammad were home again. Now the house was full of women. Uncle Hamza called from the mosque and Mr. Saeed talked with Mrs. Saeed. He would be taking her to the mosque to wash the body.

Most of the women left at the same time as Mrs. Saeed, but a few stayed behind to watch the children. Muhammad went into the kitchen. The counter was covered with all kinds of food the women had brought. When Mr. Saeed returned home the rest of the women left.

Mr. Saeed had dropped Mrs. Saeed at the mosque. Three other women were already waiting to help Mrs. Saeed wash the

---

[*] A pilgrimage to Makkah that all Muslims make once in their lives if they are able.

[**] Words or actions of the Prophet Muhammad, peace be upon him, which were recorded.

body. The four women all went inside the downstairs room that was built for that purpose. The funeral hearse was there, empty near the entrance, so Mr. Saeed knew his mother's body must be inside. The women would wash the body in camphored water and then wrap it in burial sheets. Then it would be taken upstairs after the noon prayer. All the people present would then do the funeral prayer.

At home it was quiet. Mr. Saeed gathered the children for a few minutes and talked about Grandma and heaven and what would happen that day. Muhammad thought his father seemed less upset. Then he thought that maybe he was just being careful in front of Fatima and Jamaal. Either way it was a relief to Muhammad.

They all had showers and got dressed in their good clothes. Mr. Saeed went to pick up Mrs. Saeed.

It was Friday, the day of gathering for the whole community at the noon prayer. When Mrs. Saeed got back she rushed upstairs to get ready. Mr. Saeed wanted to arrive at the mosque early. He called Uncle Hamza and arranged to go together. When Mrs. Saeed came downstairs, they left.

There were only a few cars in the mosque parking lot when they arrived. They entered the prayer hall and the men and boys went up to the front of the large, empty room. The women and Fatima went into the women's section. The mosque filled up quickly. People came in and did individual prayers; standing, bowing and prostrating. Then they sat down, forming long, even rows on the floor. By the time the Imam entered, the mosque was almost full.

Muhammad didn't really hear the Imam's talk. He tried to listen, but he couldn't help thinking about his grandmother.

Then suddenly the talk was over and everyone stood for the congregational prayer. The mosque was completely full. All the men stood in straight lines, shoulder to shoulder, packed from wall to wall, row after row, back to the door. The women's section was also full. The Imam stood up in front of the first prayer line and opened the prayer. Everyone followed.

After the prayer, Mr. Saeed, Uncle Hamza and Muhammad pushed their way through the crowd, back to the door, and went downstairs to carry up Muhammad's grandmother. Some men went with them and many others stopped them on the way to offer sympathy.

The simple wooden box was heavy and bulky. It was strange for Muhammad to think that it was his grandmother inside. "Not my grandmother," Muhammad corrected himself, "just her body."

When they brought the box up into the prayer hall, everyone formed into prayer lines again. There were at least three hundred people present, and Muhammad was glad because he knew a hadith about the number of people at a funeral prayer. "If any Muslim dies and forty men who associate nothing with Allah stand over his coffin, Allah will accept them as intercessors for him."

The bearers placed the box sideways, right up in front of everybody, even the Imam. Then they dropped back and joined the first prayer line.

"It's strange," thought Muhammad. "The person who dies is always put in front of everybody for the funeral prayer, even in front of the Imam. The Imam is the leader, so he's in front of all the people, but the deceased is in front of the Imam." He'd never really thought about it before, but suddenly

Muhammad understood why. "Grandma is our leader now," he thought. "She's even the leader of the Imam. She's gone ahead and every one of us is bound to follow her. Sooner or later we'll all follow."

Then the prayer was done, the Imam making dua, asking Allah to forgive Muhammad's grandmother and everyone there. As they lifted the box again, everyone took turns carrying it outside and down to the waiting hearse. Many low voices chanted, "La ilaha il Allah, Muhammadu Rasool Allah*." Then everyone got into their cars and followed the hearse to the Muslim cemetery.

Muhammad would remember for the rest of his life carrying the coffin over the thick grass and placing it on boards over the long, rectangular hole. People recited Quran as the men lowered the body down. Then everyone began shoveling in the dirt from the big mound beside the grave. Quickly, the hole filled up, people taking turns on the shovels, Muhammad taking two or three turns, working up a sweat beside his uncle, Hamza. Then they made dua and all the people began to leave.

As Muhammad walked back to the car he thought about his grandmother. "Now she knows by experience what all the rest of us only know by being told." It was as if she had crossed a border into a country that everybody had heard about all their lives but couldn't travel to. Everyone would eventually go there, but only one by one, and not return. She was all right though, she had what everyone else was waiting for.

Some people said goodbye to Mr. Saeed beside the car.

---

* There is no God except Allah, Muhammad is the Messenger of Allah. The primary article of Muslim faith.

The rest of Muhammad's family was already inside.

As the last person said goodbye to Mr. Saeed, Mr. Saeed turned his eyes to his son. Muhammad told him what he had just been thinking. Mr. Saeed took Muhammad by the shoulder and then hugged him tightly. As Muhammad reached his arms around his father's back, the pressure of his father's hug increased. Just before letting go, his father said, "Thank you."

Muhammad knew his words had struck his father deeply. It felt like when he was younger and hurt and his father had hugged him to take away the pain. Somehow the roles had been reversed. It was good, and also odd to suddenly be the one who could take away the pain.

THE SHOWDOWN

Muhammad sat up straight in bed. The room was dark and silent. He wasn't sure if he had cried out in his sleep or not, and he waited to see if he had woken anyone but himself. No one stirred. Muhammad rubbed his face with both hands. "Allahu akbar,*" he said softly. The dream was still very vivid.

He had been leaving school and the bus was very late. For some reason all the kids were going to have to walk home. The Imam and the teachers got out in front of the students and they all started walking down the middle of the street. It was okay because there was no traffic. Then Muhammad noticed that they were alone. There were no other people outside. The city was empty, the faces of the buildings looked blank and ominous. Muhammad knew that something bad was going to happen. Then he realized they were passing the place where the little boy had been shot. Muhammad could see marks on the sidewalk. There was a strange, chalk outline of the body. Everyone shuffled past, staring at the ground. Muhammad knew they were going the wrong way. He wanted to shout a warning, but the grownups were too far ahead. They were already passing the drug house. His father had told him never to go near it, but there was nothing he could do to stop himself. The crowd was milling and pushing. The building loomed, dark and broken. Shattered windows gaped black holes. Broken glass was everywhere. Muhammad wanted desperately to reach the Imam. He couldn't

---

* Allah is greater (than anything).

move though. Everyone was stopping him. Fear was swirling through the crowd. He knew what was going to happen. Why didn't anyone move? They were going to be shot!

As he sat awake, Muhammad's heart was still pounding. "Audhu bi llahi mina Shaytan irrajim[*]," he said and lay back down on his pillow. It was the second nightmare he'd had since the shooting took place near his school. He felt a little better now, having asked Allah for protection. It was only a dream. He felt all right now, having woken up. You could always wake up from a nightmare. You couldn't wake up from reality though. The drug house and the shootings were real.

Only a few blocks from Muhammad's school, a boy, younger than Muhammad, had been killed. He had been shot just walking down the street. Muhammad didn't feel comfortable anymore going to school.

The next day, at recess, Muhammad was playing basketball when a screaming patrol car shot through the side street alongside the mosque. The game stopped automatically. Everyone's eyes followed the car, their faces turned with it as it passed. The whole playground was silent. Everyone watched as the patrol car raced up the remaining two blocks to the crossroads. Muhammad was sure it would turn toward the drug house. Instead, it continued straight through the intersection and was gone.

As the siren faded, Muhammad felt the tension drain out of him. He was scared. He would never admit it to anyone, but he was scared.

Over the last six months, his school neighborhood had

_____

I seek refuge with Allah from the cursed Satan.

become a very bad place to be, and Muhammad wished desperately that someone would do something about it.

The playground was coming back to life now, but the older boys waited a moment longer to see if another car would follow. None came. The show was definitely over so they restarted their game.

"No second car," thought Muhammad to himself, "so it's not a shooting, probably not even a robbery." As he followed the basketball downcourt, Muhammad didn't even pause to consider how or why he should know about such things.

That evening, Mr. Saeed rushed through his dinner to be in time for the sunset prayer downtown.

"There's another meeting after the prayer tonight. I'll probably be home late," he told his wife.

"It's all just a lot of talk," said Mrs. Saeed. "It hasn't changed anything! It's not safe down there anymore!"

Mrs. Saeed wanted to withdraw their children from the downtown Islamic school. Three families had already done just that. Mr. and Mrs. Saeed argued about it. Mrs. Saeed was worried for her children's safety. Mr. Saeed was worried too, but his argument was, "What happens to the mosque and the school if we all just run?" Since the shooting of the eight year old boy two weeks ago, the argument had changed. Mr. Saeed was almost ready to admit defeat. It was a difficult decision for him. He wanted his children in that school. He also knew that if they pulled out, others would too. That could mean closing down the school.

"We'll see what Imam Ibrahim has to say tonight," he

said. "He had a meeting with the police again today."

Mrs. Saeed frowned and turned her back. "I have to convince him to take them out of that school!" she thought to herself. "These are my children's lives! If nothing happens tonight, I'm going to make Isa take them out."

After the Maghrib prayer, about fifty men were gathered in the mosque. They sat together on the floor in the large prayer hall.

"In the end, there's not very much the police can do," said Imam Ibrahim. "They can raid the house again, but the drug dealers will just return in a few days or move a few blocks to another building."

"What about the extra patrols?"

"They say they're already working."

"I don't see any extra cops around here! They don't care what happens down here!"

"Yeah! You think they're going to get themselves shot over us? Who are you kidding?"

The meeting began to get out of hand. Three or four men were shouting at the same time, some at each other, some at the Imam. The large circle held a lot of men whose tempers were barely under control.

"Brothers!" shouted the Imam. "Brothers. . . . Brothers! We have to keep order or we can't get anything done!"

"Nothing ever gets done anyway!" said one man from across the circle.

Imam Ibrahim let that comment pass. "If everybody signals me when they want to speak, I'll recognize you in order," he said. A number of hands shot up. "Wait just a second," said the Imam. "First we should hear from Brother Umar since he's in charge of mosque security."

"There isn't much to say," started Brother Umar, "except what I always say. The police can't really help us. It's not a police problem, it's a neighborhood problem. Most people in this neighborhood have given up, that's why the druggies originally moved in here. The police can't change that, it's up to us."

"So what do we do?" asked one man out of turn.

Imam Ibrahim called on another man.

"I say we go over there and just tell them to leave," said the man.

"That's what I say," commented Brother Umar.

"What do you mean 'leave'" called someone else. "They've got automatic weapons!"

"It's moral force against brute force," said Imam Ibrahim.

"Why not?" said Mr Saeed. "It works in front of the mosque. The druggies don't come around our street here. Why not extend that area?"

"It's easy to say," said another man, "but are we prepared to all go over there and face them down?"

"Man, I said automatic weapons!" repeated the other man.

"What are they going to do, shoot us all? We're fifty people."

"Sure, they could shoot. There's big money involved. They'll probably be high on something anyway. They're not going to be subject to reason."

"Okay, but we're fifty people. We'll know who they are. This isn't going to be any drive-by shooting. They'll have to stand against fifty people."

The circle of men became quiet.

"If we're going to do this we have to all stick together, every one of us, or it won't work," said Brother Umar.

Imam Ibrahim recited a verse of Quran in Arabic and then translated it into English. "*Surely Allah loves those who fight in His cause in battle array, as if they were a solid, cemented structure.*" He looked from face to face around the circle.

"I'm in favor of doing it," he said. "Does anyone disagree?"

No one said anything.

"It's all right to disagree," he said.

The room remained silent.

"All right," he said. "Let's go over there."

The men left as a single group. They crossed the street in front of the mosque with the Imam and Brother Umar in the lead. They passed through an alleyway, two and three people abreast, crossed the next street and went into another alley. When the Imam reached the next street he turned to face the men behind him.

"Who knows the building?" he asked.

"I do," said Brother Lamont. He worked his way up to the front.

"Does anyone else live inside?"

44

"Yes, there's an old lady on the ground floor in the back."

"Do you know her?"

"A little bit."

"Okay, you'd better come with me. I want to tell her what's happening first. Then I'll take one group with me to the first floor. Brother Umar will take the rest of you to the second floor."

"Don't make noise or any sudden movements," warned Brother Umar. "Keep everything nice and easy. We don't want to startle anyone into reacting violently. We're just here to tell them they have to leave."

"Okay," said Imam Ibrahim, "when we get to the building, Brother Lamont and I will go in first to speak with the lady. We'll come back out to get everyone else."

The group of men turned left and continued nearly to the end of the block.

The drug house was an old row house with boarded up houses on either side. There was no lock on the front door. The Imam and Brother Lamont went inside. The hallway was without lights. A lone, dim bulb burned above on the first floor landing.

It was dark back under the shadow of the stairs. They could barely see the apartment door in the darkness. Brother Lamont knocked. They could hear a TV inside, suddenly turned down. Brother Lamont knocked again. After a moment a sharp pitched voice said, "Who is it?"

"Mrs. White, it's Lamont DeWitt, from the next block

over," said Brother Lamont.

There was a pause. "What you want?" said the voice.

"I'm here with Imam Ibrahim from the mosque around the corner. We want to talk to you for a second."

There was a pause while Mrs. White stood thinking. She recognized Lamont's voice but she wasn't sure she should open the door. With the hall light out she couldn't see anything through the peep hole.

"Who you with?" she asked.

"I'm with Imam Ibrahim from the mosque around the corner," repeated Brother Lamont.

Mrs. White began to undo the bolts. She decided to leave the heavy chain on just in case. As the door cracked open, a shaft of light fell into the hallway. Brother Lamont moved into the light so Mrs. White would recognize him.

"Mrs. White," he said, "This is Imam Ibrahim." He stepped aside and let the Imam into the light.

"I'm sorry to bother you . . ." began Imam Ibrahim.

"I know you, you Martha Preston's boy."

"That's right," said Imam Ibrahim, surprised.

"I recognize you even with that beard on." She almost asked about his family but changed her mind. "What you want?"

"A group of us have come from the mosque to move the drug dealers out of here. There won't be any violence," he added quickly. "Still, it's probably best you stay inside."

"I ain't going no where," said Mrs. White. She eyed Imam Ibrahim for a moment, and apparently decided he wasn't completely crazy. "God help you to do it," she said and closed the door.

"That's just what we're counting on," thought Imam Ibrahim. "That's all we've got to count on."

When Imam Ibrahim and Brother Lamont came out of the hallway, they motioned to the waiting men on the sidewalk and started up the stairs. Brother Umar had already split the men into two groups. Mr. Saeed found himself standing right behind the Imam on the first landing, while Brother Umar and his group continued upstairs. Despite everyone trying to be silent, it was an old building and the stairs made a lot of noise.

"The people behind that door already know we're here," thought Mr. Saeed.

All the men were crowded onto the landing and stairs. Behind the door the apartment was silent. If anyone had been outside in the street, they would have seen the apartment's lights go out. Imam Ibrahim knocked.

"Who's that?" called a voice from the apartment, inside, away from the door.

"It's Imam Ibrahim from Al Aziz Mosque and some of the brothers. We've come to tell you you have to leave this place."

There was silence and then the voice came again in an incredulous tone. "What you say?"

"I said, you're going to have to leave this place. We've come to move you out."

There was a high pitched laugh and then some muffled talking inside. "Get out of here before I blow you away!"

"We're fifty people," said Mr. Saeed.

Silence.

"Open the door," demanded Imam Ibrahim.

"The first one touches that door gets a full magazine!" said the voice. There was more muffled conversation inside. "We ain't coming out and you ain't coming in, so you might as well go home."

"This is our home," said Imam Ibrahim. "This is our neighborhood. We'll stay right here all night if we have to. We won't hurt you," he assured them, "but we want you out of our neighborhood, and we're staying till you leave."

Now the talking inside the apartment became agitated. They could hear one man cursing at another. Then they turned as they heard the brothers from upstairs coming back down the stairway. They were escorting the men they'd found upstairs out of the building. The men they were escorting were in bad shape.

These men were not dealers, they were users. There were four of them and two could barely walk. The Muslims had to support them on either side and almost drag them down the stairs. One of the men protested loudly.

"Take them out to South Ave. and turn them loose," said Imam Ibrahim. "Explain to them that they can't come back here. They can't do what they do around here anymore."

Brother Umar had come down from upstairs, with a hard, bitter look on his face.

"You should see it," he said. "It's like a pit out of Hell up there."

"What are you doing?" came the voice from inside.

"We're sending some of your customers home," replied

Brother Umar.

"Open the door," said Imam Ibrahim.

There was silence again, except for the noise of the four drug addicts being taken out into the street. This time the silence lasted a long time. The sound of a police siren grew in the distance. The sound moved closer.

"Oh, no," said Brother Umar as he realized what was happening.

"That's the police," came the voice from inside. "We called them on you for harassing us. You better get lost, or we'll press charges."

Imam Ibrahim shook his head. "We're not leaving until you do."

When the police arrived, the drug dealers opened their door. Mr. Saeed couldn't believe what he was seeing. It was all upside down. The police talked to the dealers. Then they talked to the Muslims.

"Look, why don't you just go home?" one of the two policemen asked Imam Ibrahim.

"No," said Imam Ibrahim. "We're staying till they move out."

"They're going to file a complaint," said the policeman, almost pleading. "I'm going to have to arrest you."

"No," said Imam Ibrahim.

The policeman shrugged.

"Those three are the leaders," said the drug dealer who had been speaking through the door earlier. He pointed out Imam Ibrahim, Brother Umar and Mr. Saeed. "I saw them through the peep hole in my door."

For the second time in five minutes, Mr. Saeed was astounded. It was like some kind of bizarre dream. "Officer," he said, "these men are drug dealers, they've got guns!"

"Did you see any drugs?" asked the policeman. "Did you see any guns?"

"No . . ." started Mr. Saeed.

"Neither did I," said the policeman, "and I've been scanning this room as hard as I can without actually touching anything! Look, I know what's going on here as well as you do, but he's got a valid complaint, and I can't search for what I know is here without 'probable cause for suspicion'."

The two policemen then cleared the apartment of everyone except the dealers and the three accused. They took down the formal complaint of the dealers and then stood to go.

"All right," said one policeman. "We're going to take the three of you down to the squad car and the rest of the crowd is going to disperse. I don't want any trouble."

"Yes, we'll come with you," said Imam Ibrahim, "but, no, they will not disperse. No one will give you any trouble though."

"They will disperse!" said the policeman, losing his temper. "If they don't disperse, I'll call in more squad cars and make more arrests."

"Do what you have to do," said the Imam. "We won't move till they move." He indicated the drug dealers with a nod of his head.

The policeman kept silent. It wasn't smart to argue now.

His job now was to get downstairs and get these men into the squad car without sparking an incident. That was his main concern.

They started down the stairs. The air was thick with tension and hostility.

"It's all right. . . . It's all right. . . ." Imam Ibrahim kept repeating. The policemen were nervous, passing the angry faces that lined the landing and stairs. "Don't make any trouble, but don't leave," said the Imam. "Stay right here till those dealers move out."

They had gotten downstairs now. No one besides the Imam had said a word. The policemen were beginning to think that they might just make it outside without any trouble.

"Just what the Devil you think you doing?" A sharp voice cut the silence like a knife. Mrs. White, had pushed her way through the men that crowded her downstairs hall.

"I'm arresting these men!" announced the officer, emboldened by the previous lack of trouble. "Then I'm going to call in more squad cars to arrest all of these others, unless they disperse!"

"Disperse, my foot!" said Mrs. White. "They ain't got to disperse! This my house, and they my guests!"

The policeman shut his mouth.

"They my guests and this here my building! What you mean, 'disperse'?"

The policemen decided not to argue. They hustled the three Muslims outside and into their car. As they drove away, the officer who had done most of the talking picked up the microphone and began to report to the controller at the station house. He hung up the microphone after saying a lot of numbers and they all drove on in silence.

"I feel like an idiot," said the officer who was driving. He looked at his companion. The other officer just shrugged.

Mr. Saeed was still astonished at what had taken place. How could any sane person think this was right? Then, suddenly, he thought he saw a way out.

"Just wait till the newspapers get a hold of this," he said from the caged-in back seat. "I can see the headlines now, 'Citizens Arrested At Drug Dealers' Request!'"

"I wonder how the Police Commissioner would like that," said Imam Ibrahim, joining in.

The two policeman looked at each other with sour faces. The driver shook his head. "Like an idiot," he mumbled to himself.

Imam Ibrahim, Brother Umar and Mr. Saeed stayed at the police station for less than an hour. They were not even charged. One more carload of Muslims was brought in and then the arrests were called off. It seemed that the Police Commissioner decided he wouldn't like those headlines at all.

After another half an hour, all six men were back on the landing outside the drug dealers' door. Finally, the dealers gave up. By one o'clock they had moved out with only a few suitcases. In a cloud of curses and threats, they were suddenly gone.

By two o'clock in the morning, Mr. Saeed was back home. Only then did he fully realize how shaken he had been by the whole incident. He sat in the living room alone, thinking for a long time. When he went upstairs to the bedroom, Mrs. Saeed awoke.

"That was a long meeting," she said. "Did you get anything decided?"

Weeks and months went by and the neighborhood changed. The drug dealers all moved out. People seemed more friendly in the streets, and the atmosphere of fear lifted. Neighbors of the mosque would stop and talk to the Muslims who came for prayers. The school began to thrive again. Muhammad wasn't nervous anymore. In the Saeed household a standing joke grew out of the night 'daddy got arrested'. Mr. Saeed never joked about it though. He was as proud of that one night as he was of anything he had ever done.

TV OR NOT TV

"It's amazing. I never really looked at TV like this before," said Muhammad.

"We hardly let you look at TV at all," laughed Mr. Saeed.

"I know," said Muhammad. "It's amazing though. Abdullah's showing us all the tricks they use on people who do watch TV. He's studying media and television production in college, and he says that TV is the most powerful brainwashing and propaganda tool ever invented."

"I know," said Mr. Saeed. "That's why we almost never watch it. That's also why I'm not sure I want you going over there every evening. They've got cable too, don't they? All kinds of bad things get shown on cable."

"We're not watching cable or any really bad things," said Muhammad, "though once you know what you're looking at, just the ordinary things are bad enough. Abdullah's set it up just like a class. Look, I'm even taking notes." Muhammad showed his father the notebook he had bought.

"You're really serious about this, aren't you?" said Mr. Saeed.

"Sure," said Muhammad. "I don't want to become a slave to my desires just so some company can get rich off of me!"

Mr. Saeed nodded. "Quite right," he said. Muhammad was already talking like a college student.

"By the way, dad, those nature shows and the news you

let us watch can be pretty dangerous stuff too. If we're going to watch those shows, we should know how to analyze them."

Mr. Saeed smiled. "Not to mention analyzing the advertisements that go with the shows," he said.

"That's right," said Muhammad.

"Okay," said Mr. Saeed. "You can go, but when your course is over, I want to see what you've learned. You can show us your analysis."

"Great," said Muhammad. "They're going to pick us up from Daud's house." He started for the door.

"I'll meet you at the mosque for the Isha* prayer," said Mr. Saeed.

"Okay," said Muhammad. "Assalaamu alaykum."

"Wa alaykum assalaam**."

Abdullah was the older brother of Muhammad's friend, Lateef. He had put together a short media analysis course as a project for college. Now he was testing the course on the boys in his brother's class at school.

"Okay," said Abdullah as he rewound the video tape to the beginning of the ad. "How many lies, how many questionable statements and how many unprovable statements did you find?"

"I found three lies," said Muhammad. "It's a lie when the lady says the fake bacon tastes just like the real one. The fake stuff's made out of turkey. I've never eaten bacon, but even I

---

* (E-Sha) A night prayer in congregation; one of five prayers a day for Muslims.

** And upon you be peace; the answer to the Muslim greeting and goodbye.

56

know that turkey and bacon don't taste the same. Then the man lies when he says his wife's a genius just because she bought fake bacon. Then he lies again when he says it's the best invention since they invented breakfast."

"I got four," said Mustafa. "The product itself is a lie. It's turkey that they make look, taste and smell like something it's not. They call it 'Bacon Beater' when it's only processed turkey."

"How about the dancing?" asked Abdullah.

"Yes," said Daud. "Bacon just does not dance! Not even fake, processed turkey-bacon can dance!"

Everyone laughed.

"I've got another one," said Lateef. "The whole commercial itself is a lie. The man and woman aren't married, and those children aren't their children. They're all only actors paid to make you buy something. It's all a lie."

"There were lots of questionables and unprovables too," said Muhammad. "How can you prove that you're 'miles ahead in taste'? It doesn't even mean anything."

"I liked when she said 'two slices are as good for you as this glass of whole milk'. What does that mean? In what way is it good for you; protein, vitamins, cost, taste, cholesterol?"

"Here's one I bet none of you even know about," said Abdullah. He started the video tape again and froze it on a close-up picture of breakfast on a table. There were eggs and bacon and toast on a plate. Beside them was a half a grapefruit in a bowl. There were pats of butter laid out in a little dish and a glass of orange juice beside a cup of steaming coffee. There was a vase of flowers in the middle of the table.

"Don't those eggs look nice and shiny and appetizing?" asked Abdullah. He didn't wait for an answer. "They were cooked long before this scene was filmed and were covered with glycerin to make them look fresh. If someone ate them they'd be sick. The fake bacon and the toast have probably been retouched with color and the coffee has detergent in it to make those few bubbles at the edge of the cup stay there. The butter's made of plastic. If anyone actually ate that meal it might kill him. By the way, those flowers are fake too, so they couldn't even be used at the poor guy's funeral."

All the boys laughed. Muhammad couldn't believe it. "You mean all the food that looks so great in all those commercials is faked?"

"That's right," said Abdullah. "It's a total hoax."

"What about magazine advertisements and billboards?" asked Mustafa.

"They're all faked," said Abdullah. "The real thing doesn't look good enough, so they manufacture something that does. It's just a lie to make you buy. You know those photographs where some liquid is pouring into a glass?" he asked.

"Sure," said Daud. "They're usually for some kind of alcohol."

"Right," said Abdullah. "Well, that's not really liquid. What you're looking at in those photographs is molded, colored plastic. The ice cubes are always plastic too. There are special artists that make their living just arranging, treating and faking all the food you see in advertisements. There's a famous case where a maggot infested turkey was used to make a beautiful, thanksgiving dinner, turkey commercial."

"So much for truth in advertising," said Lateef.

"Advertising has nothing to do with truth," said Abdullah. "It's the art of making something, anything, look like it will change your life; if only you buy it. It will make you happy, successful, carefree. You will never be bored. You will be fulfilled if you only buy this!"

Abdullah looked at his watch. "That's it for tonight," he said. "It's almost time for the Isha prayer. We'll have to cover the kids' commercials tomorrow. Then we'll get into children's programming and daytime TV."

Later, driving home from the prayer with his father, Muhammad shook his head in disbelief. "It's amazing!" he said.

Mr. Saeed glanced at his son. "How was the class?" he asked.

"Incredible!" said Muhammad. "Did you know that if you ate the food used in a TV commercial it would make you sick? They put all kinds of stuff on it to make it look good for the cameras. It might not even be food at all. It's unbelievable what they get away with, to make you buy something! They spend hundreds of thousands, even millions of dollars on just one commercial!"

"Then the commercials must be effective, or they wouldn't waste so much money," commented Mr. Saeed.

"You bet they're effective," said Muhammad. "It's brainwashing! The people who make them study psychology to use on their potential customers. They can make people want what they don't need, and need what they don't want!"

Mr. Saeed laughed. "Is that a quote from your teacher?" he asked.

"No," said Muhammad. "It's a quote from an advertising executive!"

Mr. Saeed shook his head. "There's another sentence you could add to that," he said. "They can also make people buy what they can't pay for. Not just individually, but as a whole country. Everyone keeps so busy earning and spending and trying to pay back what they already owe that they hardly have time to think of anything else. Most people are completely stuck in that cycle. They get trapped in this world with no thought of the next. They end up wasting their lives."

"Did you know that TVs are considered a necessity of existence by the government?" asked Muhammad. "Even if you go bankrupt, you get to keep your TV."

"No thanks," said Mr. Saeed. "If I ever go bankrupt, they can have it."

The week's course went quickly. Abdullah covered everything from children's cartoons to late night talk shows. At the end of the week, Muhammad felt like he'd had a blindfold taken from his eyes. Before, he had thought of TV as just idle entertainment. Now he thought of it as a calculated assault.

"It's a battle for peoples hearts and minds," said Abdullah. "You must realize that everything on TV is minutely calculated and precisely executed for maximum effect. Nothing exists within a production, no dialogue, no background, no props, nothing that has not been intentionally put there to produce a response in you."

The final days of the course were spent making presentation tapes so the boys could show their families what they had learned.

That next evening Muhammad stood in his living room with the TV beside him. He had his tape in the VCR, ready to start, and his family was just settling down for the presentation. He had practiced all weekend what he was going to say. When everyone was quiet he began.

"Welcome to the land of infinite desire," he said. "It's a land where you will be taught to want and to worship money, power, women or men, and, of course, shiny new merchandise. It is a land that teaches you to worship these things through trickery and deceit. The sole purpose of this land is to change your thoughts and your behavior so you will buy what is sold here. Billions and billions of dollars are spent in this land simply to control your mind. Welcome to a land where no one is safe, least of all small children. Welcome to TV land.

"In the Quran, Allah warns us ...

"'*Then, do you see such a one as takes for his god his own vain desire? Allah, knowing, has left him astray, and sealed his hearing and his heart and put a cover on his sight. Who, then, will guide him after Allah? Will you not then receive warning?*'

"This is a warning that can be applied directly to the viewer about the purpose and effect of television."

Then Muhammad began the tape. As he went along, he

stopped it again and again to point out the tricks and techniques being used. He analyzed both the obvious and the hidden messages being sent to the viewer. At one point he asked his little brother, Jamaal, a question.

"Do you remember that racing car toy you saw on TV and wanted so badly?"

"I don't know," said Jamaal.

"It was the one that you pumped up with air and then pushed the button to shoot it off," explained Muhammad.

"Oh, yeah," said Jamaal.

"It wasn't as big as you thought it was, was it?"

"No," said Jamaal. "It was tiny. It didn't even go half way across the room!"

"It broke during the first week, didn't it?"

Jamaal nodded.

"I'm going to show you how they make those toys look so good. They do it with camera tricks and actors. They can make a toy look big when it's small and fast when it's slow. They can make it look really sturdy, but to make one commercial, they might break twenty toys. Then they pay kids to look like they're having fun when the toy isn't fun at all."

When he was finished, Muhammad launched into a look at the overwhelming use of "magic" as a theme in both programming and commercials. Then he changed the subject again and asked his father a question.

"Would you invite a murderer into our house?"

"Of course not," said Mr. Saeed.

"Would you invite adulterers, half naked people, thieves,

drug addicts and psychopaths over for the evening?"

"Of course not!"

"Well, if you watch television, that's exactly what you're doing. In day time talk shows you get the real people who do those things, in night time TV you get the dramatizations. Either way you fill your house with people you would ordinarily stay as far away from as possible. The result is a kind of corruption. People think it's all right because it's only TV. That corruption sells products."

Muhammad finished the presentation with an overview of violence.

"How many murders have you seen in your life?" he asked his sister Fatima.

"None," said Fatima.

"How many armed robberies have you seen, mom?"

"None," she said.

"How many rapes and assaults have you seen, dad?"

"I've only seen two assaults, thank God."

"So, if you add up all the years each of us has lived on the planet," Muhammad looked down at the pad where he had done the calculation, "you get ninety-two. In ninety-two years of living we have all only seen two physical assaults. In one day of watching network television last Saturday, I saw nine murders, six assaults, twelve robberies, a rape, a lynching and two riots. That's not including the assaults in cartoons, which were too many to count. Also, we only had one TV and had to keep changing channels so I'm sure we missed a lot. We didn't use cable and we didn't include the violence that was talked about but not shown. We stopped our viewing at eleven o'clock. Violence is promoted, because violence sells."

Muhammad wound up the whole presentation with a sobering fact.

"Today, television has become the primary educator of the children of the U.S.A. By the time the average child graduates high school, he or she has watched more than twenty thousand hours of TV. That's two and a third full years of nonstop television."

"That's frightening," said Mrs. Saeed.

"The frightening thing is that people are being controlled and they don't even know it," said Mr. Saeed.

"I didn't like the part about all the violence," said Fatima.

"I liked the Big Wheels," said Jamaal. "I bet that wouldn't break like my race car."

Mr. Saeed looked at Jamaal. He could see that his son was on the verge of asking for what he'd just seen on TV, even though he knew it was fake.

"I think it's about time we put the television away for good," said Mr. Saeed.

PRECIOUS

Mustafa laughed. "Your great grandfather must have been quite a man," he said. Muhammad had been telling Mustafa some of his family history. "I would have liked to have been there when he showed up at the court and got his land back."

"So would I," said Abdullah. The two boys were sitting on the bleachers at the playing field of the high school near Muhammad's house. They had come up through the woods, crossed the park, and were now watching the high school track and field team practice. They were eating oranges.

"It's interesting too," said Muhammad. "The side of the family that tried to steal my great grandfather's land lost all their own land in one generation. My side of the family still has their land. The people who tried to steal lost everything."

"Sometimes you lose everything anyway," said Mustafa. "Did I ever tell you about my family?"

"No," said Muhammad.

"They were slaves," said Mustafa. "We only go back to my great great great grandfather, Sippio. He was brought over from Africa as a boy on a slave ship. We don't know anything beyond him. We do know he was Muslim though."

"He was Muslim?"

"Yes, though no one knew it until my father became Muslim. Then, all of a sudden, some of my Grandmother's memories about her great grandfather made sense. He was a really old man when she was a little girl and she remembers him praying by putting his forehead on the ground."

"But why wasn't your family Muslim after his time?" asked Muhammad. "Didn't he teach his family Islam?"

"We don't think he knew that much Islam himself," said Mustafa. He was only nine or ten when his whole village was captured by slave traders. He survived the African stockades and the slave ship, but his parents and sisters didn't. Most of the slaves didn't. When he grew up, he taught his family what he remembered of Islam, but it was only bits and pieces. By the time those pieces got down to my father's generation, they were just looked on as family customs. For instance, our family has always said 'in the name of God' or 'I begin in the name of God' whenever we did anything. No one knew where that came from, except that Grandaddy Sippio used to say it. Later, when my father became Muslim, he realized it was part of Islam. There's another big thing that lets us know Grandaddy Sippio was Muslim."

"What's that?"

"His name."

"Sippio? That doesn't sound like a Muslim name."

"No, Sippio was the name given to him by his owner. Slaves couldn't keep their own names. They were given new names by their masters. Sippio was the name of some Roman general. But Grandaddy Sippio used his own name secretly with his wives. It came down through our family as 'Mustifay'."

"His name was Mustafa!" said Muhammad.

"Yup," said Mustafa. "I was named after him."

"You said he used his name only with his wives," said Muhammad.

"That's right," agreed Mustafa. "He had more than one wife."

"The slave owners allowed that?" asked Muhammad.

"They wouldn't have," said Mustafa, "but they didn't know about it."

Muhammad put another piece of orange in his mouth and chewed. He thought about being allowed or not allowed to do something by your owner; about being given a name on a whim; about being bought and sold. It wasn't something he'd really thought about before, not in personal terms. Muhammad's own ancestors had been conquered by the British in India and ruled over by them for hundreds of years. That was one kind of slavery, Muhammad supposed, but it was a very different kind than Mustafa's family had gone through.

"Grandaddy Sippio had two wives," Mustafa continued. "One was my great great great grandmother, Sarah. My whole side of the family comes down from her. The other wife's name was Precious. We never even knew that until recently. We only found their side of the family three years ago."

"This is getting confusing," said Muhammad.

Mustafa laughed. "Okay, he said. I'll start from the beginning.

"When Grandaddy Sippio landed in Charleston, he was put up for public auction and bought by a planter named Yates. That was in the mid eighteen hundreds, about a hundred and fifty years ago. Grandaddy Sippio was a smart boy and the planter liked the look of him, so after a couple of months in the fields Sippio was moved inside as a house servant. He was taught to serve and run errands and even to read and write his name and some simple words. He was a lot better off than the slaves in the field.

"Grandaddy rose to be second in charge of the house slaves. A white overseer was in charge of all of the slaves on the plantation, but the house slaves were dealt with directly by the masters, so they had their own internal chain of command. My grandma remembers her Grandaddy Sippio as a very old man, talking about that time as his 'golden age'. He was very bitter and sarcastic about it. She says he almost despised himself for thinking that they had treated him well.

"Precious was a servant girl growing up in that same house.

"Grandaddy Sippio fell in love with Precious when she was still a girl. She was already beautiful, and as soon as she became a woman he asked Yates for permission to marry. Yates hesitated, but Mrs Yates thought it was a good idea. They only had four happy months together.

"Precious was soon pregnant. Grandaddy Sippio thought that her sudden nervousness might be because of that, but he was wrong. Yates was showing interest in her. At first it was just remarks and looks, but it soon graduated to touching. Yates always did it secretly so Mrs. Yates never knew. Precious was terrified. She was this man's property. He owned her! She was terrified of what would happen, but she was terrified of telling her husband too. She was afraid he would try to kill their master. If she told Mrs. Yates, she would be whipped for lying and sold out to the fields of another plantation, and what about her baby?

"Grandaddy Sippio used to find Precious awake and crying late into the nights. Her almond shaped eyes, so pure and beautiful a few months before, became trapped and frantic, full of fear. She refused to tell him what was wrong. Then one day,

70

Yates ordered Precious to bring him something in his office. He had never done that before, it wasn't even her job. Mrs. Yates was sick upstairs.

"Precious went to the kitchen. Quietly, she sat down, looking straight ahead. Her face was a set mask of fear. There was no way to escape the master. Her eyes fell on a large carving knife.

"'Why, what's the matter child?' asked the cook, looking at her.

"Precious didn't answer. She just picked up the knife and cut her own face twice, from cheekbone to chin, down across her upper lip. The cook jumped forward, screaming. Precious dropped the knife and began to wail. Blood was everywhere. When Grandaddy Sippio arrived, the cook and servants were holding Precious back against the chair with towels against her face. She was fighting, but they were holding her back. When they held the towels aside for Grandaddy Sippio to see, his eyes looked like someone had taken the knife to his heart.

"'She did it herself,' said the cook. 'And I've seen the like of it before with this master!'

"Grandaddy Sippio's head snapped back as he suddenly understood. A strangled sound came from his throat. He looked from side to side like a trapped animal. He stood up, clenching and unclenching his hands. Then he ran from the room bellowing fury.

"He probably would have killed Mr. Yates if he had thought to take a knife. But he was a house slave, not a field slave, he knew nothing of fighting. As it was, he was dragged away from choking his master by Yates' two sons and Jacob, the head slave. He was flogged nearly to death.

"Three days later Grandaddy Sippio was sold as a field slave, while Precious, still on the Yates' plantation, was cutting cotton in the sun.

"Precious hardened to her work and her face healed with long, thick scars. Her soft young beauty was replaced with the hard flesh of necessity. When time came to give birth, she left the field in labor and was back working the next day with the nursing baby strapped to her. She had made trouble in the Yates' house and was shown no kindness.

"Grandaddy Sippio hardened too. He was kept for clearing land, logging and rail splitting. It was a large plantation and he lived in one of the cabins for the single men. This new plantation was not far up the Savannah river from the Yates plantation, but there was no news about his wife or child, and no way to get it.

"The house and field slaves rarely mixed with one another. Though Grandaddy Sippio had been a house slave and knew the house slaves of his new plantation from past visits with Yates, he was now a field slave. House slaves and field slaves did not mix. Worse yet, he was a trouble maker and not to be mixed with by anyone who valued their position. Any news the house slaves might have known stayed with them. Grandaddy Sippio resigned himself to never seeing or hearing about his wife and child again. He withdrew into himself and became a quiet, somber man.

"Those first months were terribly hard and lonely for Grandaddy Sippio. He wasn't used to the work or the harsh treatment of the overseer. He wasn't used to field life. He found it hard to make friends. Months passed and finally Grandaddy Sippio remarried. He married my great great great grandmother,

Sarah. She was a field slave like Grandaddy Sippio and after they married, they built and shared a small shack with another slave family. They built the cabin at night.

"Only night time belonged to the slaves. In the day they did the master's work, all day, from first light to after sunset. At night they did their own work, building, washing, cooking, sewing, repairing. Even funerals and weddings had to be held at night. About the only thing of their own the slaves could do in the day time was give birth, and that only because the masters hadn't figured out how to control it yet. Sarah gave birth to a boy in the day.

"That first child from Sarah gave Grandaddy Sippio great joy. He felt like he'd gained back some of what had been taken from him. He began to smile again. They were the first smiles the other slaves had ever seen on his lips. At night, when the infant woke for milk, he would take the baby from his wife and look at it and think, 'You're my child. You're my two children in one now.' With the change in him, it was just that much worse when the summer fevers came and the baby died.

"All that day, working in the forest, felling and barking trees, Grandaddy Sippio thought of his dead baby boy in the cabin, his dead two babies. His first child was also gone, as dead to him as his son in the cabin. All day Sippio used the axe and wedges, placing his feet and chopping automatically, all the time feeling the life had been taken out of him and killed. When night came, he put together a little box from pine scraps and put the baby inside. Sarah felt like screaming and tearing her hair for her lost baby, but she was too terrified. 'We'll have more,' she said over and over to the deaf ears of her husband. He didn't listen, he didn't care. Then Sarah began to wail. The other women joined in and Grandaddy Sippio carried the little box out alone, no need of bearers, past the rows of shacks.

"The people joined behind him, some singing hymns, some wailing, some chanting things in forgotten languages. The torch-lit mob moved slowly down the track to the bank of the river and along it to the slave cemetery. The hole was dug, the box lowered in and the dirt shoveled back. Everyone went home, everyone except Grandaddy Sippio. He wouldn't talk to anyone, so they just left him, sitting in the grave yard, looking at the river. He thought he might throw himself in. He thought it might be better. He stared at the water a long time.

"A sound came clear across the water. It was a hollow sound, wood against wood. Grandaddy Sippio woke to the sound as if from a dream. There was a boat out there. There was only the light of the stars, but Grandaddy Sippio thought he saw it for a second, moving downstream, and then it was gone.

"Grandaddy Sippio stayed by the graveyard all night, sometimes standing and bowing and putting his forehead on the ground in the half forgotten Muslim prayer. Then just before dawn the boat came back. This time the quick, strong rowing sound of oars against gunwales came unmistakably across the water. Grandaddy Sippio left the graveyard and followed the river path, leaving the main path to the slave quarters. He was careful not to make any noise. He heard the rowing sound clearly, and every once in a while thought he glimpsed the dark form of the boat on the water. When he reached the cottonwood grove, he lost the sound.

"Grandaddy Sippio stopped at the edge of the trees where the great sweep of open lawn led up to the main house. He listened but couldn't hear a thing except the gentle sucking of the river. The working dock was further up with the warehouses and road leading to it, but the small dock was only a hundred yards across the lawn. Grandaddy Sippio waited.

"He heard the man coming before he saw anything. There was the sound of bare feet pounding on the mud of the track and quick breathing. Then he saw the dark form, bent low, coming toward him, just about to enter the trees. When Grandaddy Sippio grabbed him, the man jumped to the side and almost screamed, strangling back the cry in his throat. 'Lord!' he gasped. It was Aesop, one of the single slaves. 'Lord God, save me!'

"'Quiet!' hissed Grandaddy Sippio. 'What were you doing?'

"'What was I doing?' whispered Aesop. 'Lord! Sippio, is that you?'

"'With the boat,' added Grandaddy Sippio. 'What were you doing with the boat?'

"'What boat?'

"'Don't play with me, or I'll tell them!'

"'Lord, don't tell them, they'll flay me alive!' Aesop grabbed Grandaddy by the forearm. 'Promise you won't tell nobody!' he said.

"'Promise,' said Grandaddy Sippio.

"'I went downriver, visiting. Windemere.'

"Grandaddy Sippio's breath came out in a rush. He knew it! He'd known it the moment he heard the boat. Windemere was further downriver than the Yates plantation! 'Why?' he asked.

"'My family's there. Lord, Sippio, it's getting light out!'

"Grandaddy Sippio looked at the sky. Dawn was spreading from across the river. He let Aesop go. 'You go straight back,' he said. 'I'm coming in from the graveyard.'

"'Don't tell!' gasped Aesop and he took off at a run.

"For the next few days Grandaddy Sippio was strangely calm. His wife, Sarah, found him somehow contented and his presence soothed her in her own distraction. Yes, they would have more babies, he said. On the third day, Grandaddy Sippio was gone all night.

"Aesop dropped Grandaddy Sippio on the river bank above the Yates warehouses.

"'You come back for me!' said Grandaddy Sippio.

"'You just make sure you're here,' said Aesop. He looked at the sky. 'When that dipper's gone halfway down, you be here!' He shoved off back into the current.

"Grandaddy Sippio made his way quickly up to the slave shacks. Precious would be in one of the single women shacks, but which one? Maybe she had married again. No, Grandaddy put that thought out of his head. How could he find her? He picked the nearest married shack and slowly pushed open the door. It made a loud scraping sound.

"'Who's that?'

"Grandaddy Sippio closed the door before he answered. 'Sippio.' The shack was silent. 'I come to see Precious.'

"'They'll kill us all, if they find you here!'

"'I'll kill you now, if you don't find me Precious!'

"'Wait.' Feet padded across the earthen floor. The man was standing right in front of Grandaddy Sippio now, face to face. 'You brought a load of trouble down upon yourself already, don't you bring one down on us, too!'

"'Take me!' said Grandaddy Sippio.

"'No,' said the man. 'Wait . . . Rachel!' he whispered.

Another pair of feet padded across the floor. The man and his wife spoke in whispers for a while and then she slipped outside.

"Now Grandaddy Sippio was trapped. If the woman betrayed him he would be caught, a runaway. Just when he'd decided to flee, the woman slipped back inside with another figure behind her. It was Precious."

"Subhanallah!*" said Muhammad. "Did they run away?"

"What?" said Mustafa, "and leave my great great great grandmother, Sarah?"

"Oh," said Muhammad. "I guess not, or else you wouldn't even be here, would you?"

"There wasn't any place to run to anyway. How do you run away hundreds of miles with your faces clearly marking you as slaves? No, they stayed. Grandaddy Sippio raised two families."

"You mean he just kept visiting at night?"

"When he could," said Mustafa. "They had seven kids together. Grandaddy Sippio had nine more with Sarah. That's sixteen in all."

"And he never got caught?" asked Muhammad.

"Not until the Civil War, when most of the white men were gone and he got too careless," said Mustafa.

"Then what happened?" asked Muhammad.

"He got traded again," said Mustafa.

"Oh, no!" said Muhammad.

"Then Sherman's army came and set them all free," said Mustafa. "That army destroyed everything in its path, but they did set the slaves free. Grandaddy Sippio found Sarah and her

---

* All glory is for God.

78

family, but he never found Precious. He never saw her or her children again."

The boys were walking beside the track now, heading back toward Muhammad's house.

"So, how did you ever reunite with that lost side of your family?" asked Muhammad.

My uncle Adam's become kind of a super detective," said Mustafa. "Every year we have a big family reunion, and Uncle Adam spends all year long writing letters and placing newspaper ads, trying to discover parts of the family we don't know about. Three years ago he found the Precious side of the family. Last year we had about a hundred and fifty people at the reunion and it just keeps getting bigger."

"Subhanallah!" said Muhammad. "I thought my family was big!"

"A lot of the girls on that side of the family are still named Precious," said Mustafa. One of the great uncles is named Mustifay. They didn't know anything about Grandaddy Sippio being Muslim either, until we told them. Since then, my great uncle, Mustifay, and most of his family have reverted back to Islam."

"You said your family lost everything, being brought over here as slaves, but it looks to me like you're finally getting some of what you lost back."

"That's true," said Mustafa. "but we're the fortunate ones. It reminds me of the photograph of the original Precious we have now. It's one of those real old black and white ones with scratches in it. She's very old in that picture, sitting ram-rod straight in an old chair. You can see the two scars on the side of her face. She looks like a really tough old lady, but unbelievably sad."

The Children's Stories Project

Director:
   Dr. Omar Hasan Kasule

Coordinator:
   Dr. Kadija Ahmed Ali

Advisory Panel:
   Sharifa Alkhateeb
   Nellie Jones Al-Saigh
   Susan Douglass
   Sarah Kasule
   Kalid Tarapolsi